JAN   2020

S0-BIJ-792

Copyright © 2016 by Clay Rice
All rights reserved.
Published by Familius LLC, www.familius.com

Familius books are available at special discounts for bulk purchases for sales promotions or for family
or corporate use. Special editions, including personalized covers, excerpts of existing books, or books
with corporate logos, can be created in large quantities for special needs. For more information, contact
Premium Sales at 559-876-2170 or email orders@familius.com.

Library of Congress Cataloging-in-Publication Data
2016937302   ISBN 9781942934684

Cover and book design by David Miles
Edited by Lindsay Sandberg
Artwork created using papercut silhouettes and digital textures.

10 9 8 7 6 5 4 3 2 1   Printed in China   First Edition

CHARLESTON COUNTY LIBRARY

ANTS 'N' UNCLES

I had an uncle who just couldn't dance, although he tried so hard

'Til one day, he stepped in an ant bed while walkin' through the yard.

He hiked up his pants and started to dance, his feet kicked high in the air.

We watched wide eyed as
he'd shuffle and slide,
just like Fred Astaire.

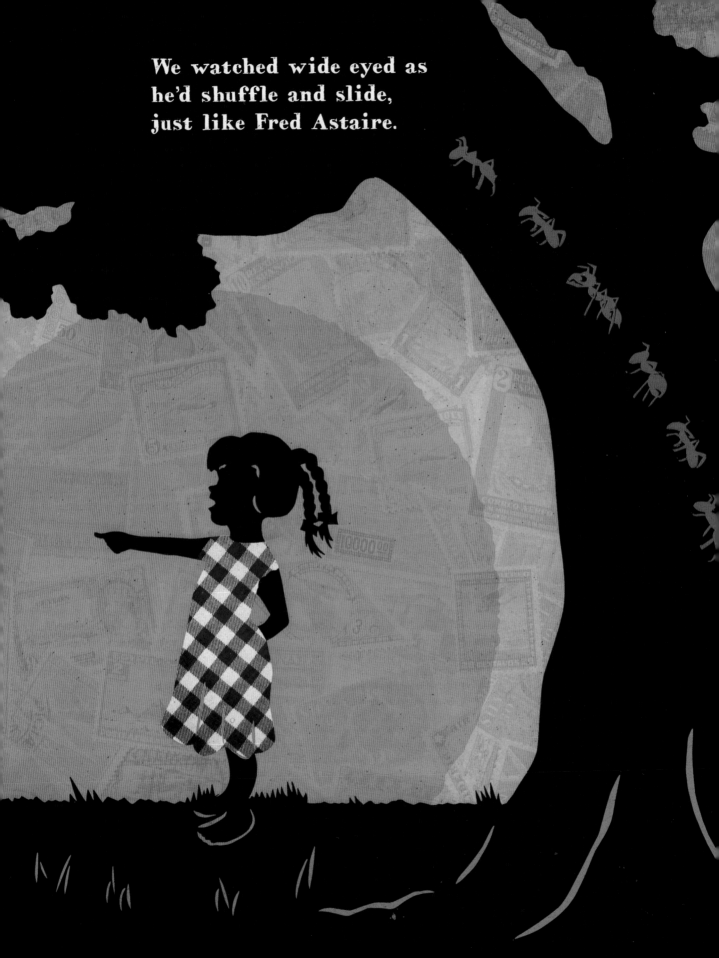

He danced right through the neighbor's yard and sashayed down the street.

He disappeared over the hilltop, but he never missed a beat.

Ants 'n' uncles, uncles 'n' ants, dancin' the world with ants in his pants.

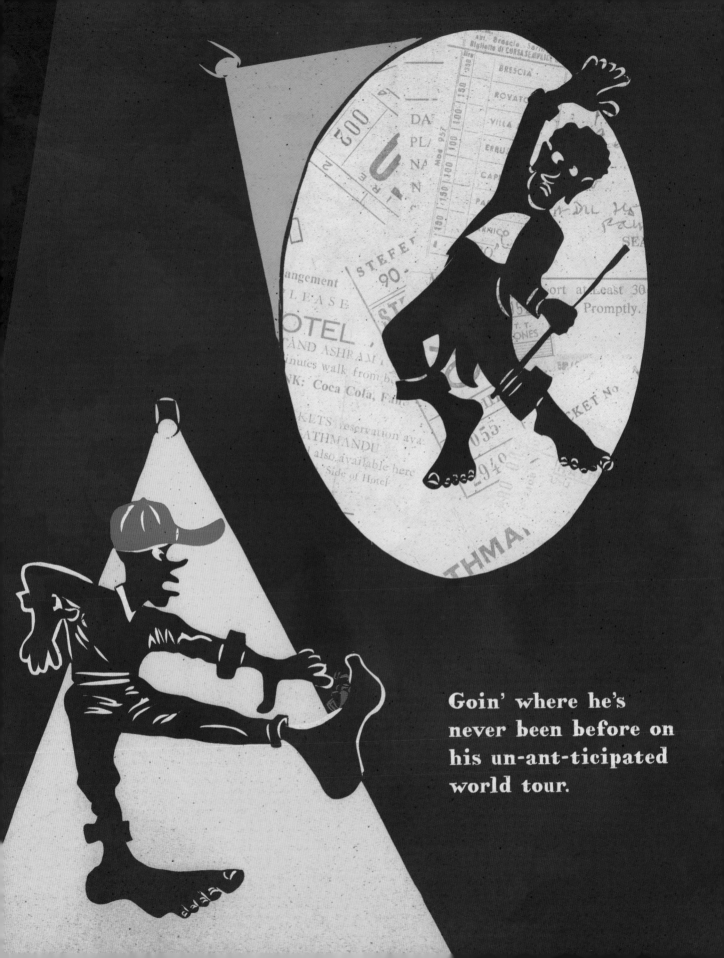

Goin' where he's never been before on his un-ant-ticipated world tour.

He two-stepped through
TEXAS

Merengued
through

MEXICO

He loco-motioned across the ocean
And limboed under mango trees

He stole the scene and France's
heart when he pirouetted in

PAREE

He moonwalked through

MOSCOW

And cut a rugga in

CALCUTTA

Then he tangoed back through

RIO

He's really something to see!

Oh . . .

Ants 'n' uncles, uncles 'n' ants, dancin' the world with ants in his pants.

Goin' where he's never been before on his un-ant-ticipated world tour.

He's so sophisticated,

His dances
agitated,

exasperated,

underrated,

ANT
ANIMATED!

Now he is the world's greatest dancer;

He's in all the magazines.

I have to read the newspaper just to
tell you where he's been.

Well that was last spring when he learned to dance, and now it's almost summer,

So if you see my uncle, tell him . . .

. . . he's three months
late for supper.

Ants 'n' uncles, uncles 'n' ants, dancin' the world with ants in his pants.

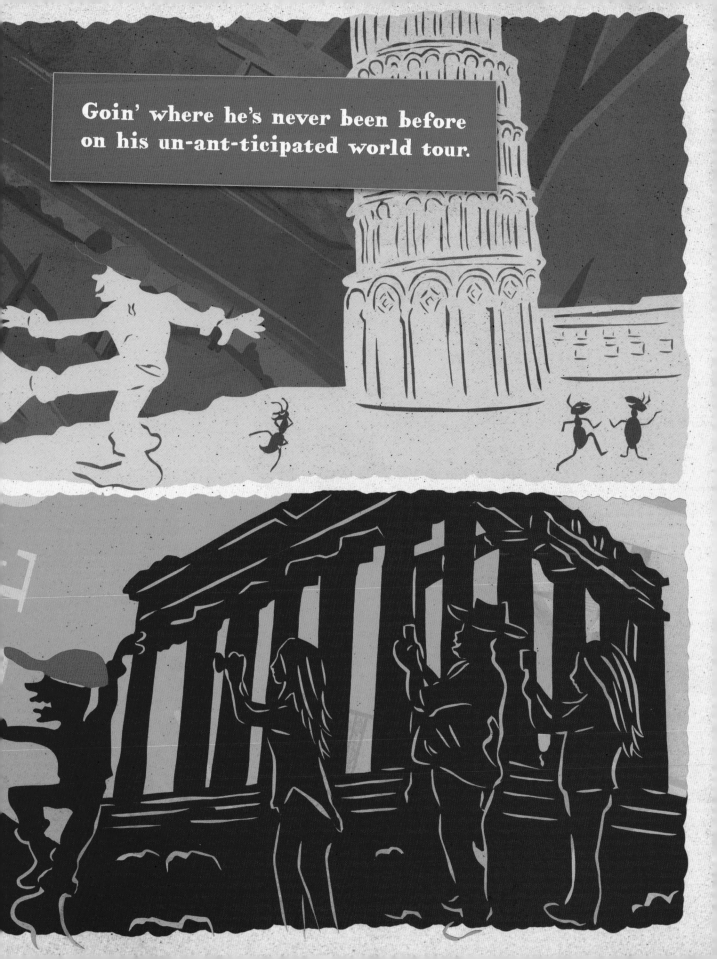

Goin' where he's never been before on his un-ant-ticipated world tour.